JUST RUN

JUST RUN

Deb Loughead

James Lorimer & Company Ltd., Publishers
Toronto

James Lorimer & Company Ltd., Publishers acknowledges the support of the
Ontario Arts Council. We acknowledge the financial support of the Government
of Canada through the Canada Book Fund for our publishing activities. We
acknowledge the support of the Canada Council for the Arts for our publishing
program. We acknowledge the Government of Ontario through the Ontario
Media Development Corporation's Ontario Book Initiative.

Cover Image: iStockphoto

Library and Archives Canada Cataloguing in Publication

Loughead, Deb
        Just run / Deb Loughead.

(Sports stories)
Issued also in electronic format.
ISBN 978-1-55277-699-5 (bound).--ISBN 978-1-55277-668-1 (pbk.)

        I. Title. II. Series: Sports stories (Toronto, Ont.)

PS8573.O8633J88 2011   jC813'.54   C2010907609-5

James Lorimer & Company Ltd.,   Distributed in the United States by:
Publishers   Orca Book Publishers
317 Adelaide St. West   P.O. Box 468
Suite #1002   Custer, WA USA
Toronto, ON Canada   98240-0468
M5V 1P9
www.lorimer.ca

Printed and bound in Canada.
Manufactured by Friesens in Altona, Manitoba, Canada in August, 2011.
Job # 67905

For my friend, Ann Christin Larsson

CONTENTS

1 THE CEDARVALE "WORMS"

The starting pistol goes off, and every muscle in my body reacts. The first runner on our relay team charges from the starting line. My adrenalin starts to pump — almost like blowing air into a balloon. In seconds Mary's slapped the baton into the second runner's hand, and Ella takes off.

I suck in my breath and watch Ella round the curve. Everyone is watching from the sidelines, too, but it's all a blur to me. Ella has to make a perfect pass to Samantha, the third runner, and her twin sister. From where I'm standing, as team anchor, I can feel that balloon of tension expanding in my chest. Will Samantha even reach me this time?

And then I hear it. The sound you never want to hear when you're running a relay race. The clank and clatter of the baton hitting the track. The balloon in my chest pops, and I feel myself deflating yet again. Samantha stops running, turns around, and shuffles slowly back to the spot where she fumbled the baton.

It's the same spot where Ella is standing, hands on her hips, shaking her head. Meanwhile the rest of the girls we've been running against, the grades six and seven teams, have gone thundering past us in their lanes. Coach Polito is at the finish line, either congratulating them or telling them how to improve their time. I jog towards my teammates.

"You're not concentrating, Samantha! What is your *problem?*" Ella yells loud enough that practically everyone on the track and field team can hear her.

Samantha stamps her foot and points a finger at her sister. "Well maybe if you'd get it right in my hand for a change instead of just slapping my fingers with it!"

"I so did *not* do that," Ella tells her.

"Alright, cool it!" Coach calls as she wanders over from the finish line. I haven't had a chance to cross that line yet today.

"Tough break, Daze."

I turn to look over my shoulder. Finn Sinclair, the anchor on the boys' relay team, is standing there beside the track, his deep brown eyes looking sympathetic. Suddenly my legs, the ones that were pumped to run a couple of seconds ago, feel like a couple of limp noodles. I try to stay composed.

"You said it," I tell him. "I can't figure out what's going on with those two. They used to be so dependable, but lately Samantha and Ella are blowing every pass. I'd love to actually finish a race today for a change."

By now Mary has wandered over, shaking her head. Coach has reached us now, too. I don't like that grim look on her face and the way she's raking her fingers through her thick, salt-and-pepper curls.

"Don't you have something you should be doing? Like warming up, maybe?" she asks Finn as she reaches us. "Don't distract your teammates, okay?"

"Sure thing, Coach," Finn says. He shoots me a sheepish grin and wanders back to the rest of his team.

"You too, Cole," Coach tells Finn's teammate. "Unless you have some advice on passing the baton that you'd like to offer all of us. Because whatever technique Ella and Samantha have been using hasn't worked today." She glares at the girls and their eyes focus on the ground.

Cole has been beside Ella ever since the baton hit the track. They're standing so close that the skin on their arms is practically glued together.

"Samantha actually has to close her hand on the baton," Cole says in a solemn voice, like he's solved the problem.

"Oh, like I didn't know *that* already," Samantha snorts back at him. "Thanks for the news flash, Cole! Maybe if Ella would get it right, then —"

"Quit blaming Ella," Cole tells her as he lopes away.

"Enough already!" Coach is shaking her head and rolling her eyes. Everyone on the field is watching her now, waiting to hear what her next instructions will be.

"Take a break, girls. Let's have the boys' teams in position now. I want all of you on the track, grades six to eight. Make it snappy."

Mr. Jensen, her assistant coach, starts rounding up the boys' teams from the sidelines where they've been waiting for their turn to practise. The rest of us girls plop down in the grass and start pouring water down our throats. I gulp from my water bottle and watch Finn. He crosses the field into position on the track as fourth runner, just like me. Oh, if only he would actually LIKE me!

"Daisy? Snap out of it." Mary is nudging me with her running shoe, stretching out one of her long legs.

"Snap out of what?" I say to her, pretending I don't know what she's talking about. But already I can see that she's followed my gaze in the direction of Finn. "And anyway, you're looking, too," I remind Mary. "Don't even try to deny it!"

"Whatever," she says, grinning. Mary's about five foot ten in bare feet. When she runs, her long chestnut hair streams out behind her like a veil. And her toffee-coloured skin is the envy of all the girls. It's almost as if she has a perma-tan!

I try to fluff up my wavy black hair. It's pretty much pointless though. My short hair matches my short, compact frame. I've given up the dream of ever growing as tall as some of my friends. Short and speedy . . . that's me!

"He's a cutie," Samantha pipes up. "Kind of a Justin Bieber thing going on, right? It's impossible *not* to stare."

Ella is shaking her head and rolling her eyes.

"I don't get you guys at all," she says. "What do you see in him anyway? It's Cole by a mile for me. I mean, check him out. He's so pumped, he makes the rest of his team look like little weenies."

Ella is practically drooling. Her eyes are following Cole, Finn's biggest running rival, even though they're on the same team. Finn is fair and tall and lean and easygoing. And Cole is the opposite: stocky, dark, and muscular, with a pirate look and matching attitude on the track. He looks way older than fourteen, and acts it sometimes, too.

Cole never enjoys losing, so having Finn as competition this year hasn't exactly been working well for him. It always used to be all about Cole. He won all the races and was athlete of the year for his grade. But now the spotlight isn't on him anymore. The fact that Cole and Finn are on the same relay team complicates matters even more. You have to respect your teammates — that's what a team is all about.

The vibes between Finn and Cole are totally negative. They avoid talking to each other, which doesn't work well when you're on a team. Sort of like Ella and Samantha. In fact, ever since Finn showed up at our school this year and cleaned up against Cole on the track, nothing has been quite the same on the grade eight relay teams, both guys *and* girls!

"Are you kidding me?" Samantha frowns at her sister. "Cole is so *passé*. You should just forget about him."

"He is *not* passé," Ella says. "He's so *cool*. He reminds me of Johnny Depp."

"Johnny *Depp*?" Samantha looks over at me and rolls her eyes, then sticks her finger in her mouth and makes a gagging sound. "More like John Travolta in *Grease*!"

We all crack up when she says that. Except for Ella, who gives her sister one of those if-looks-could-kill glares. Then Ella tosses her head and turns her back on all of us, clearly missing any humour in Samantha's joke.

"Wow, you two just don't agree on anything these days," I tell them. "And Coach is starting to notice that it's affecting our races. So you guys had better figure it out. Soon, too. Like in time for the meet next week. Or the Vipers are doomed."

"We don't need a lecture from you, too, Daisy," Ella snaps at me.

"Alright already," I tell her, then look over at Samantha. She just looks back through wide blue eyes and shrugs.

Some people find it hard to tell Ella and Samantha apart, since they're practically clones. They're not quite as tall as Mary, but nearly. Both are blond and blue-eyed, with freckles sprinkled over their cute, turned-up noses. I can tell them apart though because Samantha has a tiny red birthmark shaped like a heart on her left calf, and Ella doesn't. Besides, their personalities are different, too, which you discover once you get to know them well.

We've been pretty tight all through school, the four of us. We've been on the track team together at Cedarvale Middle School ever since sixth grade. A winning combination of relay runners with me as the anchor. We even trained together in a track club all winter so that by spring we'd be in our prime. And it worked, because we're the fastest at school and we've kept our team together.

In the city-wide meets last year we came in second. It was a major letdown for all of us because we were sure we'd given it our best effort. But like Coach Polito says, there's always room for improvement. And this spring my goal is to be standing on the top step of that podium. But with the way things have been going lately, I'm starting to get a little worried.

I realize that we're all staring at Finn now. Finn realizes it, too, because he's waving at us from where he's waiting in his lane for the starting pistol to go off. Ack! I'm mortified. He's looked right into my eyes! How can he *not* know I'm crazy about him? And maybe, just maybe, he likes me too! Is that even possible?

"Did you just *see* that? He was looking *straight* at me, and he actually *waved*! I'm dying here!" Mary swoons back onto the grass.

"Are you kidding? He was *so* looking at me," I tell her.

"He was not, Daisy," She gives me a shove with her cleated track shoe.

"You guys are such losers," Samantha says. "He was totally looking at Jazz!"

Jazz Bunting. Of course. She's the girls' 2000-metre superstar. The four of us are sprinters, but Jazz could run forever. She always wins cross-country meets in the fall and distance races in the spring. She's cool-headed and competitive, with a sweet personality and looks to match.

"Oh, come on, he was so *not* looking at me." Jazz yanks out a handful of grass and tosses it in Samantha's face. "Why would he even look at me with the rest of you sitting here?" She's humble, too. And a big fat liar!

The other members of the boys' relay teams have all gotten into position on the track. Langdon and Josh are both out there now, too, the second and third runners for the grade eight team, while Wyatt, the team sub, watches from the sidelines. Wyatt got bumped down to sub this year when Finn was faster than him during time trials. Total drag for Wyatt. It wasn't good for Cole, either, since now he's only the second fastest on the team. It's great for the team, but a real blow to Cole's massive ego, that's for sure.

"Hey! You four Vipers!" Coach is waving at us from midfield and she doesn't look impressed. "Why aren't you warming up? You're not *nearly* ready for next week.

Just *run*, will you! Get *moving*!"

When our coach says get moving, you move!

Within seconds we're back on our feet again and start practising hand-offs in the grass beside the track. If you don't get the hand-off right, you're sunk. It's the key to a good race. Sometimes even if you're not the fastest team on the track, you can make up time with a perfect hand-off. The trick is not to fumble the baton.

We're trying our best to master a "blind hand-off," where you don't even look over your shoulder. You just wait for the baton to slap into your palm before you take off at full speed. It's a matter of connecting, waiting for that moment when your teammate yells "stick" and your hand is stretched out behind you ready to grab it. It's so hard not to look, though! So we practise constantly.

We just don't seem to be in sync these days. There was a time when the four of us operated like clockwork, as Coach put it. Our timing and our passes were perfect. But in the last few weeks we seem to keep messing up. Especially Ella and Samantha, who aren't in tune like they used to be. It's almost like they're working against one another. No use in pointing fingers, because with everything that's been happening at home lately, I'm just as much to blame as anyone else on the team.

And what good is a team without some major teamwork going on? Right now it's missing from the

Cedarvale Vipers. We even had team t-shirts made with a coiled viper silk-screened on the back, jaws wide open, ready to strike.

The way it's been going this year, though, might as well be a picture of a worm!

2 EVERYTHING COULDN'T BE WORSE

Dad is on the computer when I get home after track practice. This is not unusual.

Ever since the economy took a nose-dive and he lost his job in computer Information Technology last year, he's been hunched in front of his laptop all day long. The money they gave him in the severance package is almost all used up, and he really needs to think about finding a new job soon. I'm not sure what he's doing out in cyberspace, but I'm pretty sure it's not job hunting. And all I really wish is that he'd join the real world again.

Whenever I step inside the door each afternoon, he disappears. It's as if the instant he hears my key turn in the lock he leaves the room, like he doesn't want me to know what he's doing online. I have my theories, but I haven't shared them with Mom yet. She's too busy to listen anyway, since she's an RPN, a Registered Practical Nurse. She spends most of her time at the health clinic where she works because there's always a shortage of staff.

Mom, the family breadwinner, is just carrying on with her life as usual, pretending there isn't a problem. But I know it's driving her crazy. *Because god forbid he should start dinner himself, or even throw in a load of laundry*, as she likes to say. Mom's totally frustrated with the situation, and I don't blame her one bit.

"Hey Dad," I call out as I drop my backpack in the front hallway amidst a pile of shoes and other random junk.

"Hey Daisy," he calls back to me. Dad chose my name himself, since his favourite book has always been *The Great Gatsby*, for some reason. Daisy was one of the main characters in that novel.

As I step into the kitchen he's already slinking down into the basement to hide out. Do I dare ask him what he's up to, yet again? Chances are he'll have the usual comeback for me: *Not much.*

"What's for dinner?"

"Not sure yet." His voice is muffled now. "I think your mom mentioned that she's bringing in some takeout."

"Again?"

"Um . . . Oh yeah." There's a pause. "Maybe that was Friday."

I swear he's totally losing it! "Yes Dad, that *was* Friday. Is Nate home yet?"

"I'm not sure. Didn't hear him come in."

Then he's not home, obviously, because if he was, Dad would have vanished by now. Nate, I figure, is at play rehearsal. He's totally obsessed with the drama club this year. I have a feeling it's more like a raging hormone thing for him though. He's part of the stage crew, and doesn't have an actual role. But there are so many girls in the play that for a twelve-year-old in sixth grade, it's the best place to hang out after school a couple of times a week.

I start rustling up some leftovers. There's chicken left from Sunday dinner yesterday, and about a cup of gravy. I toss the chicken and gravy into a pot to warm up and add a can of mushroom soup. Next I'll toss in some frozen peas, heat up the whole mess and serve it on toasted buns for Dad, Nate, and me. Presto. Chicken à la King.

Chances are Mom won't make it home in time to prepare anything herself. She's usually late at least four nights a week, so if we wait for her we won't eat until ten. If we're lucky. A few minutes later Nate slams through the door and drops his stuff.

"I am starving to DEATH," he groans. "Please tell me that there's something for dinner tonight!"

"I'm on the case, kiddo," I tell him. "'Cause I'm sure Mom will be late, yet again."

"What's up with that anyway?" Nate says, frowning. "She's, like, never here anymore. And how about Dad, chilling in the cellar all the time. He hardly ever even talks to me these days."

Uh oh. Nate is starting to notice too. "I'm sure he

has a lot on his mind," I try to reassure him. "You know, trying to find a job and stuff."

"He *lives* in front of the computer," Nate says, sliding into a chair and leaning forward on his elbows. "And he's the one who always complained when I used to do that. Did you notice he disappears as soon as we get home? Heads straight for the basement, like he doesn't want us to see what he's doing."

I sure don't want my little brother stressing out over this, too. And I know the best way to distract him is with food and girls.

"Don't worry about Dad, Nate. It'll all work out. I'll have something ready for you to scarf down in about ten minutes. So how's the play coming along anyway? Is that girl Sadie that you have the hots for in the cast?"

Nate just rolls his eyes and glowers at me. Then he heads for the stove, lifts the lid off the pot, takes a long sniff, and smiles. My plan worked.

★ ★ ★

Mom shows up late for dinner, as usual. By the time she's rattling the key in the lock it's after ten. I'm eating a bowl of cereal and watching a *Seinfeld* rerun when she flops down into an armchair in the living room.

"Where's Nate?" She looks around the room as if he might be hiding somewhere. Ever on the alert for her kids, like a nervous mother cat.

"No hello or anything, Mom? He's in his room, probably playing video games."

"Sorry, Daisy," she says, then comes over and plants a kiss in the middle of my forehead. "I should be thanking you for looking after things around here. Any dinner left? I'm starving!"

"You mean you haven't even eaten yet? There's some mush left on the bottom of the pot on the stove, but I'm not sure it's edible by now." I explain to her how I rustled up leftovers to create a meal, like I've seen on TV, and she's practically salivating.

"I'll pop it in the microwave," Mom says. "I only had time to grab a muffin and a coffee around six, and that wasn't nearly enough. The clinic was so busy they needed me to stay later than usual. Some kind of virus going around. Huge lineup of patients all day long. I'm exhausted."

"You'll get sick too, Mom," I warn her. "You're not taking good care of yourself. Jeez, I'm actually starting to sound like you!"

Mom laughs as she wanders into the kitchen. Then I realize that she hasn't even asked where Dad is. There's a sudden little twist of fear in my gut. I've been dwelling on some scary thoughts about Mom and Dad lately that make me feel sick inside. And I have to keep running away from them before they catch up with me and my brain goes into overdrive. If that happens I won't be able to focus on anything else.

"How was track practice, anyway?" she calls from the kitchen. "Is that amazing relay team of yours still holding together?"

That's when I turn off the TV and take my empty cereal bowl into the kitchen.

"It's okay," I tell her as I rinse the bowl in the sink. "Could be better, but we're working on it. Don't put any dirty dishes in the dishwasher. It already ran. I'll empty it in the morning."

"Honey, I promise I'll empty it when I'm done eating." Mom grabs me by the shoulders and gazes into my eyes. It's like looking into a mirror. I don't even have to wonder what I'll look like some day, I just have to look at my mom. "Honestly, you're doing such a good job around here, helping out with everything." Is that a real tear, or are her eyes just watering? "Sometimes I feel so guilty."

"Don't feel guilty, Mom." I give her a quick hug. "Sometimes Nate even helps me. He cleaned up after dinner. He just forgot to empty the pot. Or *chose* to forget."

"I'll clean it up after I eat," Mom says as she scoops the reheated hash onto a couple pieces of toast. "This looks delicious."

We hear thumping footsteps on the basement stairs and her eyes narrow.

"Is that the troll that lives in the dungeon downstairs?" she whispers just as Dad appears in the doorway.

"Oh, hi Diane, you're home. I didn't hear you come in." Dad's eyes look tiny and bloodshot, probably from all the screen time.

"So? Any luck *today*, Glen?" Mom's voice has an undeniable chill to it that I don't like very much. Clearly Dad doesn't either, because he's standing there frozen in his tracks. Then he shrugs, like he's trying to pretend her tone doesn't bother him.

"I'm checking the job websites every day, but there's nothing new. And I've sent in applications, but nobody ever calls me back." Then his shoulders slump. "It's tough going out there. Nobody seems to be hiring."

"Well we're really getting short of money now. We can barely make the house payments, not to mention all the other monthly expenses. You've got to find something soon, or we're doomed." She heaves a huge, weary sigh as she starts to eat.

Dad stands there staring at her back for a moment. He blinks his eyes slowly, sadly. Then he shakes his head and shuffles out of the room.

"Mom?" I sit down at the table across from her and try to catch her eye. "Is . . . is everything okay? I mean, with you and Dad? With . . . everything?"

By the look in Mom's eyes when they finally meet mine, I can tell that everything is definitely *not* okay. In fact, everything probably couldn't be much worse.

★ ★ ★

It's hard to concentrate at school when your family life is a shambles. Hard to stay awake, too, when you've tossed and turned half the night and fought off dreams of your Mom leaving for work one morning and never coming home. But that's exactly what happened to me on Monday night. I can't get the thought out of my mind, and I actually have a few frightening dreams of our house with Mom gone. Me, Nate, and Dad walking around with hollow eyes, dragging our feet, a bunch of zombies who can't function.

I manage to get through all my classes on Tuesday morning without actually snoring.

But then I feel myself nodding off during French class as our teacher drones on about *passé composé*. Yawn! French grammar is as boring as watching grass grow to begin with. But Madame's dull voice could work as well as any anaesthetic in an operating room.

She warns me once by calling out my name and asking me to repeat what she just said. And I can't, so I know that I've been in that grey space between awake and asleep. I'm getting pretty good at leaning on my elbow, chin perched on my hand, trying to look alert while I zone out for a while. But I think some of the teachers may be onto me!

That's what I like about running so much. It's freeing, in a way. You have to focus only on what you're doing. You can't think about anything else, especially during a relay race. It's all about timing and making sure you grab the baton and pass it on at the correct moment. Anything can screw up the race. A fumble, a misstep. Every split second counts in a relay race.

And that's why I find myself watching the clock every afternoon during the spring track and field practices. I can't wait for that bell to ring so I can leap into my shorts, my Vipers t-shirt, and sneakers and start warming up. Running is such a great distraction.

On Tuesday after school I'm one of the first on the track, jogging to warm up, doing a few wind sprints. Then when the girls show up we start practising with the baton. The other athletes drift onto the field, the long jumpers and shot putters, the high jumpers, dragging out their huge mats and clanging poles. And the distance runners like Jazz Bunting, of course, who have the stamina to run around that track for ages. Sometimes I envy that ability.

Coach Polito and Coach Jensen are wandering from group to group, checking times, asking questions, or doling out suggestions, depending on the circumstances. Our practices start out the same way every day. Coach Jensen is a new teacher at our school this year. He isn't scary at all. In fact, he always seems to be grinning and positive. Coach Polito is your best friend if you do things right. If not, well, maybe you shouldn't even be on the team. She offers words of encouragement, words of advice. And now and then words that make you want to work even harder.

Coach Polito is stalking towards me and the girls where we're practising blind hand-offs. She does *not* look thrilled, and I steel myself against the lecture that's sure to be coming.

"Has anyone seen Finn Sinclair?" she yells before she even reaches us.

Whew, at least it's not us this time. But Finn? Not again. That can't be good.

3 RUNNING INTO PROBLEMS

"Oh no." Mary looks at me wide-eyed. "Don't tell me he's late again. Coach is going to be *so* pissed at him."

The same thing happened one day last week, too. Finn showed up about fifteen minutes late for practice and got the silent treatment from Coach Polito. He also got a warning lecture that being late wasn't an option. It's not fair to keep the rest of your teammates waiting. Only committed team players get to play on the team. Something like that anyway. And Finn just stood there staring at his gigantic feet in his humongous Nike running shoes, turning red right up to the tips of his ears. Which made me wonder — if he was so embarrassed about being late, why did he do it in the first place?

And today he's done it again. That seems weird.

"Nope, haven't seen him," Ella calls out. Coach spins on her heel and walks off in the direction of the high jumpers to ask them the same question.

"That seems weird," Mary says, and I grin at her.

"I was just thinking the *exact* same thing. You know,

sometimes we're just so in tune, aren't we?"

"I was just thinking *that* exact same thing!" Mary grins back and we high-five.

"Oh *barf*, you two," Ella says. "You think *you're* in tune, try having a twin sister. We can practically read each other's minds."

"And right now you're thinking, *God, I wish Cole would run right up to me and grab me and plant a huge, wet, mushy kiss on my lips*, aren't you, El?" Samantha says with a wicked smile. Sure enough, Ella's eyes are following Cole's muscular form as he circles the track.

"Now that would be totally amazing," Ella admits, keeping her eyes locked on Cole as he rounds a curve and jogs towards us.

"You are so freaking lame," Samantha groans. "How can you even *like* that guy?"

"Hey," he says as he passes us, and flicks his wrist in a sort-of wave.

"Oh, I am *so* gonna die," Ella says, swooning.

"Not till you practise your hand-off a few more times! You're so distracted, you missed it twice today. Focus on *us*, Ella! On your teammates! Not on Cole!" I always lecture my teammates when they slack off. And they usually just roll their eyes.

"Okay, okay, control freak!" Ella says, rolling her eyes, and we all take up our positions to practise hand-offs.

A few minutes later Finn shows up. We see him jogging from the school doors across the field towards our coach. The four of us have all stopped practising. Just like practically everyone else on the field. We're all watching this little drama unfold. There's some major hand waving going on, and head nodding and shaking too. And voices are raised. Then Finn turns around and walks back into the school.

"Uh oh," I murmur. "That can't be good."

"Okay Wyatt, you're up," Coach calls to the relay sub. "Finn won't be joining us today."

Cole offers Wyatt a high-five as they head off to get into position on the track. And is it my imagination, or does Wyatt look almost uncomfortable when Cole slaps his hand? I watch Finn as he shuffles away. He takes a quick glance over his shoulder before disappearing through the doors. When I look back at Ella and Samantha, they're glaring at each other. Strange. Very strange.

★ ★ ★

Track practice just wasn't the same without Finn there. Well, I guess it probably worked for Cole and Wyatt, since they were in the spotlight for a change. But Finn just brings so much to the track and field team. He always has such a positive attitude. He's always a team player. So being late for a practice is completely out of character for him. Which makes me wonder even more.

I walk home by myself after school instead of taking

the bus with the others. It isn't that far for me anyway, and it's sunny and warm. And even better, I spot Finn at the plaza as I'm going by.

He's talking to some guys in front of a convenience store. When he sees me, he waves. Yes, he actually waves at *me*. My insides turn to mush. Then, he calls my name. "Hey Daze!" He starts loping towards me in that cool, fluid way of his.

"Hey Finn," I stammer out. *I love it when he calls me Daze! God, try not to look so flustered, Daisy!*

"So how was practice today?"

"Great. What happened to you anyway? How come you were late again? And how come you left?"

Finn glances towards the plaza where the other guys are standing as if he wants to be sure we're out of earshot. Then he looks back at me and sighs.

"Actually, it's for the dumbest reason. So dumb that I didn't want to tell Coach, or anyone else. You wouldn't *believe* how dumb it is."

"Try me," I tell him. Then we start walking and he starts talking.

"Well, for the second time the same thing happened after school. When I get to my locker after class at around quarter to three, my lock is wrapped in duct tape. How stupid is that?"

"Duct tape? Who would wrap your lock with duct tape?"

"I have no clue. And whoever did it found the

chance between lunch and the last bell. Because at lunchtime it wasn't there. It takes me ten minutes to pick off the tape so I can get out my running shoes and stuff." Finn sighs again and shakes his head. "It's just too stupid to admit to Coach Polito. So I made an excuse, and she didn't like it."

"What did you tell her?" I ask.

"I said I had to make an important phone call. And she didn't fall for it. She said phone calls can wait, that right now the team should be my most important focus. And that I should just skip practice today since Wyatt was subbing anyway. So I left."

I stop on the sidewalk and look into his melted-chocolate eyes with the incredibly long lashes. Those yummy eyes look troubled.

"So why don't you tell her, Finn? I'm sure she'd understand."

"Because I feel stupid," he admits. "And I want to know who's doing it so I can fix the problem myself. I don't want to be a wimpy little tattle-tale. It's not like grade three, you know. I should be able to look after this myself."

"Yeah, I see your point." I nod in agreement. "And in case it happens again, maybe you can use this."

I dig around in my backpack and find the little stocking stuffer from last Christmas on the bottom. It's a teeny utility knife that slides out of a little plastic case.

"That's perfect, Daze!" He gives me a quick hug as

he slips it into his pocket. And my insides get mushy all over again. Then he walks me all the way home!

* * *

Finn's problem bugs me for the rest of the evening.

Who would be taping up his lock, and why? I have a sick feeling about it that I don't want to dwell on. I know there's a bit of resentment from the guys' relay team. They're not happy that Finn took Wyatt's spot as team anchor. But they wouldn't go that far, would they? It would be too risky, especially if Finn decided to report it to the coach.

I've heated up a couple tins of minestrone soup for dinner tonight, and added a can of kidney beans and diced tomatoes to change it up a bit. I chopped some cabbage into it, too. With some Parmesan sprinkled on top, it almost tastes homemade. I found a loaf of frozen garlic bread in the freezer, which I've heated. Perfect.

A few minutes later I've ladled our supper into bowls and set one on the table in front of Nate. He's staring at the basement doorway in a daze. Dad has taken his dinner down into the dungeon with him. He barely said a complete sentence to us, even when Nate tried to have a conversation with him. Nate looked like a sad puppy when Dad just grunted and left the room. I'm sitting there staring into my soup and thinking about it. When I look up, Nate is staring at me. "It's like he doesn't even want to live here anymore," Nate murmurs.

"Don't be ridiculous," I tell him, trying to hide the worry in my voice. "He's just preoccupied, that's all."

When Mom gets home a few minutes later we're eating in silence.

"Hi you two." She slides into a chair beside me.

"Minestrone soup's on the stove, still warm, Mom."

"Sounds great, Daisy." Her eyebrows are furrowed. "You two sure look solemn tonight. Everything okay around here?"

She glances towards the basement stairs. We can hear Dad's spoon clinking on his bowl. Then she looks at me again and I look at Nate. He just shrugs and scoops up some soup in a sullen way.

"Everything's good, Mom," I tell her. "Really. Really good."

"If you say so," Mom says, raising her eyebrows at us before she heads upstairs to change out of her nursing uniform.

But it isn't really good. Because I have even more to worry about now, what with the problems with my teammates and Dad acting so weird. And it's playing ping-pong in my brain once again when I'm lying in bed later that night.

Mom and Dad's relationship is an ongoing problem. What's Dad doing on the computer all day and why is he being so secretive about it? I'm worried sick about my parents' marriage. So many of my friends have gone through the horrors of their parents' breakups. Now they live with their mom or dad and spend every other weekend with the other parent. It all seems so complicated and depressing to me. And some of them seem to despise either their mom or their dad, as if they're looking for someone to blame for their broken families. They play off one against the other, and try to see what they can weasel in the way of guilt gifts. I just *so* don't want to be a part of that game.

Then there's Finn and his lock. Who the heck would be trying to sabotage him like that? I'm not even sure I want to know, but I'm pretty sure that I already do. And we've just *got* to perfect our blind hand-off for the relay race before the track meet next week. But Ella and Samantha aren't cooperating. They used to be so dependable, so sure of each other's next move. There's too much going on in my life right now.

No wonder I toss and turn half the night!

★ ★ ★

The next morning at school I promise myself I will stay focused in French class. I will *not* let myself doze off even though I slept so lousy again and feel as if I'm drifting in a dream. Especially after lunch, when I always get a bad case of the afternoon sleepies. And this afternoon is the same as usual. As hard as I struggle to force my eyelids open, Madame's voice is like a sleeping potion. They keep fluttering shut.

"Daisy, as-tu un problème? Es-tu malade?" Her voice is suddenly as shrill as a dentist drill. I've never heard that pitch before. Neither has anyone else, judging by the looks on their faces.

Perfect! *"Oui, j'ai mal à la tête,"* I tell her, faking a headache by rubbing my temples and looking ill. "I have some Tylenol in my locker," I add.

"Vas le chercher," she tells me, nodding towards the door.

Hooray! A brief escape into the empty hallways. I take my time getting to my locker. No hurry to get back in *there*, that's for sure. And maybe the walk will wake me up, if I'm lucky.

Out in the hallway, teachers' voices drone from classrooms where the doors are open. As I turn the corner by the gym, I hear the familiar slap-and-squeal of running shoes on the slippery floor during a basketball game, the shouts and whistles, the bouncing ball.

Then I spot her. She's standing at the end of the hallway in front of Finn's locker. And she's doing something to his lock. Suddenly there is silence from the gym and I know she hears my footsteps because she looks my way. She's gone in a flash.

I start jogging down the hallway to try to catch up with her before she disappears through the closest door. But she's fast, too, and way quieter than I am. She's wearing her school track suit, so she's obviously supposed to be in gym class right now. The floors are slippery, so I run on my toes. Besides, I don't want to attract anyone's attention in these lame shoes with the hard, noisy heels that practically echo through the halls when I walk. Why did I wear these stupid shoes today? Because I wore my plaid kilt today, instead of the grey pants, my other school uniform option. And my usual sneakers don't work well with a skirt, unless I want to look totally uncool. It's too late anyway. By the time I reach the double exit doors, she's long gone. I'm totally freaked out, because when I go back down the hall to check Finn's lock, there's already some duct tape wrapped around it. And now I know.

I know who I saw messing with Finn's lock. I'm just not sure if it was Ella or Samantha. And I can't believe it was actually one of them, one of my teammates. I'm so dismayed that my hands are trembling as I grab hold of the lock and struggle to peel off the tape that she's already had a chance to stick on. She's done a good job. It's wrapped up tight as a mummy.

"*Daze?*"

When I spin around, Finn is standing there staring at me.

4 WHO TO BELIEVE?

"Finn?" *Omigawd*, I don't like the way he's looking at me. "Finn, I can explain everything! It's not what you think!"

"You're right. I didn't think it would be *you*, Daisy. You totally faked me out with that utility knife you gave me. Why would you do this anyway? To get me kicked off the team? Just leave the duct tape, okay? I'll get it off later."

When he turns around and walks away I feel like throwing up.

"Finn. *Please* wait. We need to talk about this. I didn't do it!"

He holds up a hand as he's walking away. I know what that means. I've been shut out and there's no point in running after him. And I'm absolutely sick about it. What else could he possibly think, me standing there with his lock in my hand? I almost feel as if I really *did* do it. How can I prove to him that it *wasn't* me, when I can't even believe who it really was? How can I even be sure who it really was?

I ditch my effort to pick off the tape. By the time I finally get a Tylenol out of my locker and shake myself out of my daze, the final bell has rung. It's time to get ready for track practice. But today, probably for the first time ever, I don't feel like going.

* * *

I don't have much time to think about my problem, though, because if you don't hit the track running so you can be warmed up for practice, you're sure to get reminded by the coach, in a very loud, cringe-worthy voice! I start jogging, and ahead of me on the track I spot a familiar figure, someone I haven't seen out here for a while. Inez is back today.

Inez is our relay sub. She's an awesome runner and usually kills in the 400-metre sprint and high jump but she's been missing in action for a while. Mary has been filling in for her at the meets this season. Well, Inez hasn't exactly been missing, because we knew where she was. We just don't like thinking about it, the rest of her teammates. Nobody likes to think about that sort of thing.

Inez has been off school with mononucleosis. And we're all pretty sure where she caught it. From her ex-boyfriend, a guy in grade ten. It was sort of a parting gift from him, because she discovered she had it after they broke up a few months ago. She got really sick after March Break and had to be off school for six weeks. We're not sure yet if she'll be well enough to sub for the team. But maybe it's a good sign that she's showed up today.

"Welcome back, babe!" I'm grinning when I catch up to her on the track. It's so good to see her again. "You in training now, or what?"

"Yes! Finally." She gives me one of those wide smiles that she's famous for. "My spleen's back to normal. It feels awesome to be running again."

"Ewww. That sounds so gross, Inez," I make an icky face. "What *is* a spleen anyway, and what is it *for*?"

"No idea. You don't even know how great it feels to be awake all day long. I never thought I'd complain about sleeping so much!" She flashes another one of those smiles. "I actually missed coming to school. But I mostly missed running!"

"I know what you mean," I admit. "I don't know what I'd do if I couldn't run. I practically live to run!"

We do a couple of laps side by side until the rest of the team shows up. Mary, Ella, and Samantha come running across the field towards us, and Inez and I stop and wait for them. Mary is smiling. Samantha and Ella look grumpy. Ella veers away from us when she spots Cole on the track.

"Inez! You're here! Yay for you!" Mary says. "You feeling good now?"

"Way better," Inez tells her. "I've been going out for

little jogs in my neighbourhood at night, trying to work myself up into competition shape. So you shouldn't have to fill in for me much longer, Mary. But thanks for doing it!"

"That's a relief," Mary says. "I can't kill that 400-metre the way you do. I don't know how you keep the speed up for the whole race. I can't get the timing right. Do you start off at top speed, or save it for the last stretch?"

Mary and Inez jog off together to talk about technique. Samantha is standing nearby shuffling the toe of her running shoe in the gravel. Then she crouches to adjust the laces. She hasn't looked at me. Was it her or Ella messing with Finn's lock today? Which one of them made me mess up my chance with Finn? Why do they have to be so darn identical? And now they're both in their track suits, so even their clothing isn't a clue.

Ella is still running around the track beside Cole. She hasn't looked my way yet, either. Finn is running around the track warming up, too. Of course, he won't look at me, not after what happened at his locker. I've just got to find some way to explain everything to him and gain his trust back. Finally Samantha looks over at me and our eyes lock. I'm not sure what her eyes are telling me. She has a weird look on her face, as if she's hiding something. I know this is our chance to talk while she's alone, and I grab it.

"Come on," I tell her. "Let's do some warm-up laps

before we practise our hand-offs, okay?"

"Sure," Samantha says with a sullen face. It's like she has a perma-frown these days.

She's totally silent as we jog around the track. But every time I look at her she seems to be glancing in the direction of Ella and Cole. And grimacing.

"You're quiet today. Anything wrong?"

"Why would anything be wrong?" She's squinting when she looks at me. Is that guilt or curiosity?

"No reason." I shrug and keep running, hoping she'll say something more. "But you're never *this* quiet, Samantha!"

"Whatever," she says, and keeps running beside me. When I look at her sideways, her chin is all quivery, as if she's about to start crying. Which she does!

A huge sob bursts out of her throat like she's choking or something. When I look over at her again, she's gulping air, and a couple of enormous tears are trickling down her cheeks. I stop in the middle of the track and grab her by the arm.

"Come with me." I lead her towards the bleachers where a few students are scattered watching the practice as they wait for their friends.

"Coach Polito will freak if she catches us," Samantha says, shaking from my grasp.

"She's busy with the high jumpers. We have a few minutes." We both scramble up to the very top of the bleachers where I'm sure that nobody will be able to hear us. There are some big ears and big mouths at this school that I always try to avoid.

"So why the heck are you crying, Samantha? What's wrong?" I ask her once we've plunked our bums on the hard seats.

She's still watching Ella and Cole as they circle the track. And she looks utterly miserable. Then she sighs as she brushes away a stray tear.

"It's Ella," she says. "You won't even *believe* what I saw her doing."

My stomach does a little flip. I'm so afraid of what I might hear next.

"What? Tell me."

"It was this afternoon. A little while ago. See, we both have gym class together, and I just stepped out into the hallway for a drink at the fountain . . ."

Uh oh.

". . . and I saw Ella. Standing in front of Finn's locker doing something. And when she looked up and spotted me, she ran the other way and I ran back into the gym . . ."

Uh oh.

". . . And a few minutes later she came walking back into gym looking completely innocent, like nothing just happened. Then, when I checked at the end of gym class, I saw what she'd been doing before she ran away. And guess what? She wrapped Finn's lock with duct tape!"

"*No way*," I say, trying to act surprised.

"Why would she do that, Daisy? You don't think she did it for Cole's sake, do you? So Finn would get dumped from the team by Coach Polito and Wyatt would move up from being sub? I heard Cole say once that he *wished* that would happen. I mean, no *wonder* Finn's late for practice if he has to pick that tape off his lock to get his track stuff out. What is my sister's *problem* anyway?"

I sit there staring at Samantha and feeling absolutely sick. How could Ella do something like that?

★ ★ ★

Once we've clambered down from the bleachers and rejoined the team on the field, Samantha won't look at me anymore. She's the third runner on our team. I have to rely on her to make a perfect pass during the race. She's the one who yells "stick" at me just before smacking my hand with the baton. How can she focus when she's so upset? I find it hard to concentrate myself with everything running in circles through my mind.

All I can think about is what Samantha told me. Why would Ella do it? Was Samantha right? Was Ella really trying to get Finn in trouble, maybe even get him kicked off the team?

I fumble the hand-off a few times and cringe when Coach Polito yells at me. The third time she adds,

"Good thing Inez is almost better now. At least maybe we can count on her to save the team!" Everyone is staring when she says that, since her voice is so shrill, and I hear a few snorts of laughter. I *so* wish that the ground would open under my feet and swallow me up.

I can feel a lecture coming all through the practice. The four of us are standing at the finish line after about the tenth time we've run the race. Ella and Samantha are circling each other like suspicious alley cats. Over by the long jump pit I can see Coach watching us.

"I'm so done," Samantha says. "It's hot out here and Ella is being a total jerk today."

"Me!" Ella stiffens. "Why are you blaming me? You're the one who keeps fumbling the baton when I make the pass. It slows down our time. It's like you don't even want to be a part of this team anymore."

Samantha's eyes widen and she flips a glace in my direction, then frowns.

"Yeah, right," she says. "You're not even passing it properly. It's a *blind* pass, remember? I have to count on you to put it in my hand and make it stick! We should have this race all *locked* up for the meet next week. Get it, Ella? LOCKED up!"

Ella's eyes narrow. Then she spins around and starts walking away.

"Hold it. Don't go anywhere, Vipers!" our coach hollers. Then she starts jogging towards us and we all freeze.

"Okay, now we're toast," Mary says. "What's up with you two, anyway? Do you think she hasn't noticed the way you're acting?"

By the time Coach Polito reaches us, we've all sunk down onto the grass beside the track, waiting for the pep talk that our team so deserves.

"What is the *problem* with you guys lately?" she says, standing over us with her hands on her hips. "I mean, usually you're the ones I can count on. You're the example for all the other teams. You're in your last year at this school, and should be at the top of your form, you've been a team for so long. But I'm sensing something here. And if there's a problem, then I want to know what it is. Ella? Samantha? You two have to work together. And you always have before. If you don't start cooperating then I'm going to change your positions so you don't have to pass to each other. I'll move Mary or Daisy between the two of you so you won't have to even look at each other. And if that doesn't work, then one of you will be gone and I'll sub Inez. She's almost ready to join the team again. Are you hearing this?"

Samantha's chin is quivering. She scrubs at her eyes with a tight fist. Ella's eyes are closed, her face an unreadable mask.

"Well, *are* you?" Coach demands, and both girls nod silently.

"Good. I know you two will straighten all this out and tomorrow will be way better, and next week you'll clean up at the meet. And you, Daisy . . ."

I cringe and wait to hear it. I know I haven't been running well lately either.

"You've been fumbling, too, and you're not nearly fast enough when you take off. I need you to concentrate. All of you!" Then she looks at Mary. "Nice work. If the rest of you were as focused as Mary, you'd destroy the competition next week."

"She just has to make one pass, though," I hear Ella murmur. Mary looks at her in disbelief. What a dumb thing for Ella to say.

"What's that?" Coach says. "I didn't hear you Ella."

"Sorry Coach. It was nothing," she says to her sneakers.

"That's what I thought," Coach says. "So you'll clean up your act now. Am I right, Vipers?"

"Right," we all murmur, not even looking at one another.

"Great. That's just what I wanted to hear. Make it happen, girls," she says, then goes stalking towards the school doors.

I don't hurry to leave the field after the rest of my team wanders off. I'm still walking in circles around the track to cool down after everyone else has packed it up for the day. And I'm brooding about Coach's lecture, and about Ella and Samantha. I don't want to face anybody in the change room. I want them all to be gone by the time I get there. I have too many worries cluttering up my brain right now and I'd rather just be alone to try and sort them out.

By the time I reach the change room, I *am* alone — except for one person. I can see her feet from under the door of the bathroom stall. Ella's feet — I recognize her runners.

I figure that maybe if I hurry I can get out of there before she flushes. I don't even need to change, just grab my clothes off the hook and make a dash for it. The rest of my stuff is in my locker out in the hall. But before I can make a move, the stall door swings open. Ella is standing there, her mascara all smeared from crying.

"Ella?" I say to her in a soft voice. She swipes the tears with her fist and stares back at me. Then she opens her mouth, and again, I'm afraid of what I'm about to hear.

"You won't even *believe* what I saw my sister doing this afternoon, Daisy."

"And you're going to tell me, aren't you?" I ask. She nods sadly. I sink onto one of the benches and wait for her to tell me her own version of the locker story. She babbles on for at least five minutes.

I sit there with my mouth hanging open until Ella finishes telling her story. Or her lie, because I can't be sure which sister is telling the truth now. I don't even know *what* or *who* to believe anymore!

"That's really weird, El," I tell her when she's finished talking.

"But why would she *do* it? That's what I just don't *get!*" Ella sniffs.

"I don't get it either," I admit, because I really don't. And I'm probably more confused than Ella is, because she doesn't know what Samantha told me earlier today. "But let me know when you get it figured out, okay? Gotta run. Gotta study French. My nemesis."

And then I bolt and leave her standing there wiping her face and smearing mascara all over the place. I hurry home. My stomach is grumbling, and I wish like crazy that for once I could get there to find a pot roast in the oven and delicious smells spilling out the door as I step inside. It's a sad fantasy of mine, has been for ages.

I'm so hungry that I decide to stop at the local Tim Horton's for a ham and cheese tea biscuit. I love those things, and it'll help fill the hole until I can figure out what to make for dinner tonight.

I freeze just as I reach the door. I see something through the window that makes me want to throw up. Mom is sitting there at a table sipping a coffee and laughing. Across from *another man!* A man who is *not* Dad. A man who is reaching across the table and squeezing her hand. And the man is laughing, too. He has a wide easy smile and dark wavy hair. He's actually *hot!*

My mom is in Tim Horton's having coffee with a *hot guy* when she's supposed to be working at the clinic. My mom, who practically *never* laughs anymore. What is wrong with this picture?

5 RUNNING AFTER CLUES

I make a run for it because I'm so freaked out. Just the thought of a tea biscuit, of any food at all, makes me feel even sicker. My mom, who is always complaining about how tired and stressed out she is, who is always coming home late from work, can somehow find the time to sit and laugh with a strange man in Tim Horton's late in the afternoon. It just does *not* make any sense at all!

The only thing that makes sense right now is to run as fast as I can to get away from there and to try to forget what I saw. *Just run, Daisy!* And I do, all the way home, as if I'm being chased by the hounds of hell.

When I get home my mom isn't there, of course. Dad is already hunkered down in the basement on his computer since Nate is home. Nate's playing a video game on the TV in the family room.

"Hey!" He's looking at me with hope in his eyes. "Did you bring anything home to eat? I'm starving."

"God, Nate! You're in grade six! You're old enough to make yourself a grilled cheese or something. And there's stuff in the freezer. French fries and sausages. You're starting to drive me nuts, you know!"

"What flew up *your* nose?" He gives me the finger and goes back to the screen.

Okay, maybe I was a bit harsh, but I'm still all messed up from what's been going on all day. So awhile later, when I'm making dinner and Nate is hunched over his homework at the table, I decide to share some of it with him, sort of like a peace offering. Not the Mom part, though. I don't want to freak the poor kid out completely! But I do tell him the story of Ella and Samantha and what happened with the lock at school today.

The whole time I'm talking while I fry bologna and make the grilled cheese that Nate was too lazy to make himself, he's looking at his math notebook, as if he's pretending not to listen. He's frowning a bit as he hears the story.

"So which one of them do you trust the most?" he asks. "Who's telling the truth?"

"Wow," I say. "I haven't really thought about it too much yet. I know one of them is lying . . . But who do I trust the most? Good question, little bro. But how can I even answer it?"

"Maybe I can help," Nate says, with a strange look on his face. "And you know what? I'm betting on Samantha."

"Why Samantha?" I ask, pointing the spatula at him.

"Do you know something that I don't, maybe? People can't even tell them apart. How can you even guess at who's telling the truth?"

"Samantha has that heart-shaped birthmark, right? And she has more freckles than Ella does." Then Nate blushes. "Not that I've noticed or anything."

"Ah ha!" I grin at my brother. "You have a crush on Samantha, don't you! But why her instead of Ella?"

"It's not a crush!" Nate glowers at me. "It's not like I'm a little kid or something. It's just that Samantha is always way nicer to me than Ella is. Ella barely even knows I exist. And she's totally obsessed with Cole anyway. All she ever does is drool over him at lunchtime in the caf."

"Boy, you've really been paying attention," I tell him. "But I'm not sure you're right about who I can trust. I know these girls way better than you do."

"Whatever," Nate says. "So are we eating now, or what?"

Nate is clearly done with this conversation. The bologna and grilled cheese sandwiches are nice and brown now, with the cheese starting to ooze out around the edges. I flip one onto a plate for my brother and he starts inhaling it right away. I've even made a couple for Dad and decide I might as well take them down to him on a tray. I dress up his plate with some sliced pickles and a blob of ketchup, and even make a cup of tea. Then I carry the tray carefully down the steps so I don't spill anything. Which is why I practically sneak up on my dad; he doesn't even hear me coming.

When I see what's on the computer monitor, I nearly drop the tray! I stop in my tracks, then back up to the bottom of the stairs, my heart beating hard. He can't *really* be gambling online, can he? I stand there watching for a few seconds before I speak.

"Dad, here's your dinner," I tell him.

His hand lands on the mouse and I know that with a few quick clicks whatever he was doing on that website has vanished from the screen now. He spins around in his chair and flashes me a weak smile.

"Thanks, honey," he says. "Appreciate it. Mmmm. This looks good."

I set it on his desk in front of him. He reaches for a sandwich right away and takes a bite.

"So you've been busy today, huh?" I ask him. "Get anything accomplished? Find any job opportunities out there in cyberspace?"

He stops chewing and looks up at me. There's a string of cheese hanging from his lower lip. He blinks a couple of times.

"A few possibilities. So has your mother been coaching you in the art of interrogation, or what?" he says. He looks injured, almost as if I slapped his face.

And I almost feel guilty, as if I'm prying into his private life. But honestly! "Nope, I was just curious, Dad. Aren't you getting bored, sitting around here all day?"

"A bit, I guess," he admits. "Good dinner, Daisy. Thanks."

"Whatever, Dad," I say, then head back upstairs.

I meet my mom coming in the front door.

"You're late tonight, *again*," I tell her. "Did you have a good day?"

Her eyes can barely meet mine. What does *that* mean? After what I saw her doing today I can only guess.

"Great day, sweetie. I already ate. Think I'll have a bath now." She steps out of her comfy shoes, the ones she needs to wear because she's on her feet all day at the clinic. When she's not sitting across from a strange man in Tim's, smiling and laughing.

What is going *on* in this house?

★ ★ ★

After school on Thursday Coach Polito has all the relay teams, from sixth to eighth grades, competing against each other, just for practise. Next week's meet is a big one. The winning teams will move on to the city finals at York University. So our coach is on our cases big time. She has a way of encouraging us that some people could mistake for meanness. But it's just her way of getting us to try harder, to challenge ourselves. Every team gets to hear something positive and something negative, including ours.

"Nice start and finish. But your time was lousy. *Way* too slow! You call that sprinting, girls?" She stands there shaking her head. "And those blind hand-offs were horrible. Samantha, you nearly fumbled your baton again when Ella passed it to you. You have to concentrate! Ella, you weren't moving fast enough when Mary passed the baton to you. What's wrong with all of you this week? You're usually right on top of things!"

I have a feeling I know, and as I stand there watching Samantha and Ella take it from the coach, I wonder if they both know exactly how much I know. At different times they each glance at me, almost begging me to keep my mouth shut. I have no intention of saying a word until I figure out why the whole duct tape incident happened at all. And who really did it, Ella or Samantha?

Like Nate, I'm leaning in the direction of Samantha being the most honest one. Ella is so obsessed with Cole right now that it wouldn't surprise me at all if she was doing exactly what Samantha claimed, trying to get Finn kicked off the team for Cole's sake. I'm going to keep my eyes and ears open and look for more clues. Then, when I finally get it all figured out, I plan on confronting them both. Maybe even at the same time.

"What's up with these two, anyway?" Mary whispers beside me, as if she's reading my mind again. "They're usually so intense at practices."

"No clue," I tell her.

And that's not a lie, either. I wish I knew for sure so that I could help them solve their problem. I also realize that I'm just as much to blame as far as our team goes. Lately I haven't been concentrating the way I used to. Usually running distracts me, but this crazy week everything *else* is doing that. And I'm completely disappointed with my performance. Right now, Mary is the only team member who's truly focused. That's *not* good.

"Okay, let's try it again, one more time," Coach Polito shouts to all the teams. "Trust me, you can't practise for relay too much. And nobody is going home tonight until we all get this right and I'm happy with what I see. Now move to your positions, everyone. Focus on what you're doing and just *run*, will you?"

There are a few grumbles from some members of the teams.

"You don't *really* have a problem with that, do you boys and girls?"

"No, Coach," a few contrite voices call out.

Nobody wants to have a problem with Coach Polito. Nobody likes running laps at the end of practice when you're starving and pooped and you can't wait for a shower!

A while later, when we're done for the day and heading for the change rooms, I find myself walking behind Finn, and Langdon and Josh, his teammates. Finn hasn't even spoken to me since yesterday. In fact, he seems to be making an effort to completely avoid me, and it's tearing me up inside. How can I fix this? I've *got* to find out the truth and tell him what really happened so we can break this awkward silence between us!

Ella and Cole are walking inside together, and she's pressing her arm against his, even though he's all sweaty from running on a hot and sticky day like this one. Must be love! Samantha is trailing behind with Jazz Bunting, Mary, and me, and we're all yapping and laughing. But it's hard not to miss where Samantha's eyes are focused, burning a hole into Cole and Ella's backs, from what I can see.

The change room is bustling with girls from the team, all excited about the upcoming meet, especially the younger ones, the grade sixes, who'll be competing for the first time for our middle school. I love how the teams start to meld at this point, how everyone gets along so well as event day approaches. But not our team so much, right now. Ella and Samantha have been dodging each other. They even get changed on opposite sides of the room. Ella is making plans with Mary, from what I can overhear.

"So you're sure it's okay if I come over for help? If I don't pass this math test tomorrow my parents will be furious," Ella says to her.

"It's *fine* if you come home with me," Mary tells her. "You can even stay for dinner. My mom won't care. There's always enough food for ten people anyway. My mom loves feeding people. It makes her feel good to see people eat."

Ella laughs then calls over to her sister. "Tell mom for me, okay, Samantha? I'll call later for a ride home. Mary's gonna help me pass this test."

Samantha ignores her and stands there brushing her hair.

"Samantha, tell Mom, okay?"

"Whatever," she says, then picks up her backpack and walks out.

Mary, Jazz, and I stand there looking at Ella, and she shrugs. "I don't know what is *wrong* with her these days." Our gazes meet and she frowns at me, then her eyes flicker away. I know exactly what she's thinking. *Finn's lock*, we're practically yelling in our heads. No wonder our relay team is stinking so bad.

6 WRONG TIME, WRONG PLACE

Today I'm one of the last ones to leave the change room. The rest of my team is long gone. Mary and Ella left a while ago, heading for Mary's to study Math. And Samantha vanished without even saying goodbye to anyone. When I slip out into the hallway, the caretaker gives me a nod as he goes past pushing a huge broom along the floor.

I don't hurry home, even though I'm hungry. I'm just getting so tired of making dinner for everyone all the time. If only someone else would take over for a change. Like Dad, who would rather risk losing money on the Internet, maybe even risk losing his family; or Nate, who is happy just sitting playing video games and eating cookies. Of course Mom would rather sit and laugh with a strange man in Tim Horton's than hurry home to feed her starving family. Oh, my poor family!

My stomach is definitely grumbling a bit, though. I've done a lot of running since lunchtime. So as I pass Timmy's, I can't resist running in for a ham and cheese biscuit, which I missed out on earlier this week all because of Mom and the hot guy.

I'm standing in line with my money in my hand, and it's almost my turn, when I hear a familiar laugh, and I know that it's Cole. I'd recognize his low laugh anywhere, because all the girls seem to think it's sexy, including me, I hate to admit. When I look over, I spot him sitting at a table — with Ella!

"Hey you guys," I call out. I pay for my biscuit, take a quick bite, then hurry over to join them. "What happened to math, Ella? I thought you were going to Mary's place after school for some help."

"I changed my mind," she says without looking up at me. Ella suddenly seems to be very interested in poking at some crumbs on the table.

"Hey, can you blame her?" Cole says, holding his hands out proudly like he's a god or something. "Me or math? I mean *come on!*"

"So think you'll pass the test tomorrow, El?" I ask, ignoring Cole as I take another nibble of biscuit.

And then, nuts, I drop the whole thing right on the floor. What a waste of money!

I bend over to pick it up, hoping to salvage at least the top part of the biscuit. Then I spot it. The heart-shaped birthmark on her leg — on *Samantha's* leg, that is!

There it is, right in front of my face, that small red heart, an angel kiss, she calls it, that she's so proud of. The feature that truly distinguishes her from her sister.

Cole's huge running shoe, an expensive Kanye West limited edition, is in my face, too. I almost bump my head on the edge of the table as I stand back up.

So *that's* what's going on! Suddenly it all makes so much sense. I wonder if Samantha knows that I know that she's not really Ella at all. I can't believe she could do that to her sister. And that Cole could totally miss the fact that he's sitting with the wrong twin! It doesn't surprise me, though, since I'm sure he finds it hard to see past his giant ego. I can't believe that I was wrong about Samantha, and so was Nate. There's no way I'm telling Nate about this and shattering his secret crush.

Samantha won't look at me now, and I'm too shocked to say another word, so I make an excuse and dash.

"Gotta split! Making dinner for the fam' tonight!"

"See ya," they both say, without even looking at me. They're staring into each other's eyes now. God, Cole is a big dumb lummox! But then again, Samantha had me fooled for a second there, that's how strong the resemblance is. And they always practically dress the same. Who can tell one denim mini-skirt from another anyway? And everyone wears tank tops with their bra straps showing these days, too.

As I bolt for home, I try my best to sort out this little mystery in my mind. So Samantha saw me watching her taping up Finn's lock, and blamed Ella for it so she wouldn't take the heat from me. And Ella is upset because she saw what really happened. And Samantha is totally trying to snatch Cole away from her sister!

I wonder when Samantha plans on telling Cole who she really is. Or how long she expects to carry on the charade. But why did she tape up the lock? To get rid of Finn and get Wyatt back on the team? Is it her skewed way of helping Cole become the fastest guy on the team again, so that when he finds out she did it he'll like her more than her sister? The more I think about it, though, the more sense it begins to make.

What a great way to steal the guy right out from under your sister's nose!

★ ★ ★

Kraft Dinner with some chopped up hot dogs. That's all I can come up with tonight. And I have to admit that I feel my appetite coming back as I stir in the butter and milk. I'm alone in the kitchen. Nate left a phone message saying he was having dinner at his friend's place, and Dad hasn't come upstairs from the dungeon.

I never realized how lonely you can be in your own house. Since Dad's been unemployed, he barely even talks to anyone anymore. If only he could be doing something useful with his time, instead of what I saw him doing on his computer. Poor Dad. If only it had turned out better for him and he hadn't been downsized. If only Mom and Dad's relationship wasn't so strained right now; I'm so worried about them.

I'm all tangled up in confusing thoughts when I hear him thumping up the basement steps. His face is pasty-looking from being inside all the time and he looks sad. I can't blame him. And that's the moment I decide to do it.

"Dad, sit down. I have your dinner ready and I want you to eat with me at the table for a change, okay? I miss your company. We all do."

"You do?" Dad frowns. "I thought you were all too busy with your own lives to care about mine. Big track star that you are. And Nate with his drama. And your Mom. Why would you miss my company?" He offers me a thin smile as he pulls up a chair.

"Hmm. Let's see. Maybe because I actually *like* you, because you're my dad and you're a nice guy. And Dad . . . I'm a bit worried about you, too. Because of something I saw you doing." I set a bowl of KD in front of him.

"Saw me doing?" Dad frowns again and suddenly looks a bit nervous. "What did you see me doing?"

I have to tell him this, because it's gnawing at me. But oh god, how?

"I saw what you were doing on your computer, when I took down your dinner last night. Dad. . ." The words come out so fast that I am practically tripping over my own tongue. "I saw you playing *poker* online!"

Dad chokes on a mouthful of noodles. "*What?*"

"I saw it on the screen, Dad," I tell him, speaking

more slowly now so he'll get every word. "You didn't hear me come up behind you at first. And I *saw* what you were doing on the Net. And I'm worried sick about it!"

Dad's face is turning a hot, bright red. My own face is burning and I feel like making a run for it, I'm so embarrassed for both of us.

"Oh, honey," he says, looking up at me. "I really wish you hadn't seen that." Dad lets out a long sigh and scrubs his face with his hands. "I just got caught up in it. Some of my friends told me about it because they do it, too, and I checked it out, and the next thing I knew, I was giving it a try every day."

"But Dad." My eyes well up with tears. "People get hooked on that stuff. And they can lose all their savings. And I don't want that to happen to us. Because I'm so afraid it wouldn't end well."

"I know, I know," Dad says with genuine sadness in his voice. "And I promise you, I'm going to give it up. Starting right now. Because you're right — it's already getting out of hand. The last thing you need is a gambling addict as a father."

"Oh, I don't really think it would go that far, Dad." I pat his shoulder, feeling a bit guilty. Up to a few seconds ago I really *did* think that it could!

Dad sighs and shakes his head. I can see he's having a hard time admitting this.

"I haven't lost too much money yet. And every day

I hope that maybe I'll win some. But for everything I gain, I lose even more." Now he looks sadder than ever, his whole face sort of sagging. "*Man*, I've got to get a life. I've gotten into such a rut. You can only search job websites for so long. There's nothing out there right now."

Poor Dad! He's actually *trying!* I swoop in for a little hug and he hugs me back.

"Don't worry, something will come along eventually, Dad."

"Yeah, but I think it's time I got out of the house and started really looking. I think I should try an employment agency or something. Maybe getting caught was a *good* thing for me, Daisy." He pats my hand and gives me a wistful smile. "To be honest, I'm beginning to worry about your mom, too," he adds, and my stomach does a somersault. "She's getting pretty fed up with me. I can't blame her. I think she suspects what I'm doing online, even though she hasn't actually caught me. So it's got to stop now. Hope she doesn't give up on me completely." He chuckles softly. "You don't think she'd ditch me, do you?" He looks up at me with something like desperation.

If you only knew, I'm telling him in my head. *If you only knew what I know.* That smiling man from Tim's pops into my brain and I can't erase the image of Mom smiling, too. Honestly, poor Dad! But I don't dare tell him and make him feel even worse.

"She'd never do that to you, or to *all* of us, Dad." I plant a quick peck on his bristly cheek and turn around so he won't see the tears that I'm blinking away. Dad is an awesome guy — maybe there really is hope for him. If only Mom would realize it, too.

Mom finally shows up around 7:30 when I'm at the table doing homework. She picks up the pot with left-over KD, grabs a spoon, and starts to eat without even bothering to use a bowl.

"Where's your brother?" she says, like she suddenly remembered that he's missing.

"He's at Austin's for dinner, getting dropped off after eight sometime. Hungry or something, Mom?" I ask her as she scarfs the cold macaroni.

"Busy day, no time to grab anything at dinner. One of the other nurses was off sick so I had to do double the work. Where's your dad?" Her eyes veer towards the basement doorway. "Down there, as usual?" She can barely disguise her impatience.

"Mom, he's *really* trying," I whisper. "I talked to him about it today. He knows you're probably getting fed up with him. Please don't do anything crazy, okay?"

"You actually *talked* to him about it? He seems to totally avoid the subject whenever I'm around. In fact, he seems to totally avoid *me* whenever I'm around! I can't get a straight answer out of him, either." Mom licks the spoon and shrugs. "Sometimes I think he doesn't really even want to find a job."

"I think you're wrong about that," I tell her. "Be patient, okay? Something will come up. I'm sure of it."

"Daisy, do you know how bad it is out there for IT guys right now? There's just too many of them around. I'm trying not to do anything crazy, but sometimes drastic times call for drastic measures."

She puts the pot in the sink, runs water into it, turns around, and walks out of the kitchen without another word. And I stand there feeling like barfing as I try to figure out what she meant by "drastic measures." She wouldn't really, *would* she? She couldn't possibly ditch our whole family, *could* she? That hot guy from Tim's pops into my brain again and I shiver.

Right then and there I promise myself that I will do my best to stop Mom from totally ruining our family.

7 RUNNING AFTER ANSWERS

At school on Friday it's hard to focus on my teachers' droning voices after yet another toss-and-turn night. Every couple of hours I woke up all tangled in my sheets as if I had been running from something in my sleep. Using my usual technique, I manage to doze through most of my classes — as long as your eyes are half open, the teacher thinks you're listening. I'm not really dozing today, though, since my mind won't stop racing.

Lately I've managed to be in all the wrong places at all the wrong times. And everything I've seen is completely cringe-worthy. Samantha posing as Ella and taping up Finn's lock. Samantha in Timmy's with Cole and his mega-ego, *ugh*. And I don't even want to think about Mom and that guy she was with. Then there's Dad and his online gambling problem that he has got to fix for the sake of our family. I think I may go nuts before I get this all figured out!

I have so much bugging me that I totally avoid every one of my friends all morning. In my classes I just pay attention to the teachers — or at least pretend to. In the hallways, if I hear someone calling my name, which I'm sure I do a few times, I just ignore it and walk away quickly. At lunchtime I find a shady spot under a tree and eat by myself. Finally, Mary catches up to me as I'm strolling across the grass towards the school after lunch.

"What's wrong with you today?" she asks, peering intently into my face. "Everyone's asking, and I don't even know what to say."

"Like everyone *who*, Mary?"

"Ella and Samantha. Wyatt. And Finn."

"Finn?" *Finn is asking about me?* "What did Finn say?"

"He said you've been acting really weird lately, Daisy. That you've been doing some strange things."

"I have no idea what he means," I tell her with a sinking feeling.

That's it. Finn's given up on me. And I don't blame him. I don't say another word to Mary, because I don't know who I can trust anymore. She gives me a strange look as I turn and walk away. I'm not ready to tell her how worried I am about practically everyone I know. What will become of our relay team with Ella and Samantha working against each other? How can we possibly win if we're not working as a team?

And I miss the easygoing relationship Finn and I had a couple of days ago before he caught me with that lock in my hand. All I care about is getting him to trust me again. The whole silly crush that I have on him doesn't even matter anymore. I just want him to *talk* to me!

But how can that happen when he doesn't seem to want to be anywhere near me now, and he thinks I'm acting weird? How will we straighten this out when I seem to just keep running away from the issue myself?

★ ★ ★

Even though it's Friday and nobody can wait to get home, Coach Polito has called a track and field practice.

"What a bunch of long faces! But what did you expect?" she shouts at us when we're all outside after school warming up. "The meet is next *Thursday* and you could all be way better. We've got to improve your distances and your times. Everyone needs to improve in some way. As soon as you can *prove* that you've *im*-proved, you can go home. How does that sound? Everyone ready to improve?"

There are a few weak "yeahs" and "okays" and "whatevers" mumbled from everyone around me.

"*What?*" Coach Polito calls. "I can't *hear* you! That doesn't sound very much like enthusiasm to me. Louder, please! What are we all gonna do? All together now!"

"IMPROVE!" we all try to yell.

"Now that's what I like to hear! Real team spirit!" She grins at us because she totally knows we're faking it.

"Off you go now, positions everyone. And relay teams, we'll start with you on the track, before the one- and four-hundred-metre sprints, okay?"

Our team starts *and* finishes on the track. Everyone else has been allowed to go home, including Coach Jensen. Now it's nearly six and we're still practising, because every time we try to run a race, someone does a false start, or fumbles a baton, or makes an incorrect pass. I have to admire Coach Polito's patience. If I were her, I'd want to strangle all of us! Finally she calls us over to where she's standing by the side of the track.

"Okay, what's wrong with all of you Vipers lately? I'm getting bad vibes or something. I thought you were going to work all this out. Maybe it's time for me to shift your positions. Maybe that's the kick in the butt you need to make this work! Unless you can come up with an explanation for me. How 'bout it, girls?" She looks each one of us in the eye. Mary and I look right back at her. From where I'm standing, I can see Ella and Samantha both lower their eyes.

"Ah ha, I get it!" she says. "You sisters had better get it figured out before next Thursday, or I have news for you: you're going to lose your races. You probably won't make it past the heats if you don't solve your problem. Have a good weekend, Vipers. And show me some venom next week!"

Coach Polito turns to leave, and the four of us just stand there in awkward silence watching her jog towards the school entrance. Finally, Mary sighs.

"What's up with you two, anyway?"

Samantha stares at all of us, heads over to the grass, picks up her backpack and walks away. Ella's watching her, and I can see tears in her eyes. Oh, if she only knew what I knew! I'm sitting on this news and it's burning a hole in my brain, and I can't blurt it out! It just wouldn't be right to blab how I saw Samantha with Cole in Tim's.

"We *used* to be best friends right up until, like, last month," Ella says, watching her sister walk off and sounding exactly as if she's swallowed a huge frog.

Mary pats her shoulder as we wander over to pick up our backpacks and head for home. "Is there anything we can do to help you out, El?" she asks. Honestly, Mary is so genuinely nice — sometimes I totally envy that. But I think I have a plan.

"I dunno." Ella rubs her eyes with the heel of her hand. "Like *what*?"

"What are you guys doing tonight?" I ask her. "Can Mary and I come over or something? We could all watch a movie together. Maybe talk about our team, tell her how worried we are about the meet next week. Will you be home?"

"Samantha will be for sure," Ella says. "She's been mouthing off lately to Mom, so Dad grounded her for the weekend. Something is really bugging her. She won't talk to any of us at home."

73

Huh! I'll just bet something is bugging her!

"Does that work for you, Mary?" I ask. I open my eyes wide, pleading with her to say yes. But I'm really wondering if my scheme will solve anything. What will stop Samantha from just ignoring us and hiding out in her room? Mary looks uncertain, too. "Come on, Mary. We have to do this for the team. Coach Polito's right. We totally suck right now and I know we can do better!"

"Okay," Mary agrees. "Like what time though?"

"I need to take a shower and make some dinner for everyone," I tell them.

"How about nine-ish?" Ella says. "I *really* want to try and work this out with Samantha."

"Works fine for me," Mary says, then looks over at me.

"Great! Me too," I tell them with sort-of-enthusiasm. Deep down I'm wondering how my plan can possibly work at all!

By the time I get home after 6:30, I'm so pooped I feel like falling down inside the front door. The house is quiet. *Nobody home?*

I take a quick look around. Dad isn't in the living room or the basement. He's actually gone out someplace? I can hardly believe it. Mom's nowhere in sight either, which is nothing unusual these days. I think I'd be more surprised if she got home before me! And on the kitchen table I find a note from Nate: *Gone to chill at Austin's place. Don't know where Dad is.*

That means Dad was gone when Nate got home from school, which would have been a couple of hours ago. Where the heck did he go? Maybe out for a job interview? Hope flutters in my chest for an instant. How great would that be? Maybe things would finally start to turn around for our family.

After a quick shower I slip into my bathrobe, twist a towel around my hair, and flop down on my bed for a little while. When my eyes flutter open again at the sound of the phone ringing beside my ear, the "little while" has turned into nearly 8:30!

"Daisy, are you *ready* yet?" Mary shouts into my ear.

"No!" I shout back. "Don't yell at me, Mary. I just woke up."

"But it's almost time to go! I'm coming over now. Why were you sleeping?"

"Because I was *tired*," I tell her. "Don't worry, I'll be ready when you get here."

As I hang up the phone, the gnawing in the pit of my stomach reminds me that I haven't even eaten dinner yet. And of course there's nobody to make it for me. Where are Mom and Dad, anyway? The gnawing turns into a nervous flutter and I'm not so hungry anymore. I dress quickly, have some soda crackers with peanut butter to fill the hole, and turn on the TV while I wait for Mary to knock on my door. It's a restaurant commercial with a family sitting at a table eating together, laughing and teasing each other. How long since my own family has done that? Forever, it seems. I turn the TV off again and wait in the semi-darkness, wishing things could be different.

I actually jump when Mary knocks a few minutes later, because I've dozed off again. Talk about pooped!

8 FINDING SOME ANSWERS

Mary texts Ella when we're almost there. I envy her cell phone. I so wish I could have mine back. As we walk up to the front door, Ella steps out and closes it behind her.

"Okay you guys, this isn't going to be pretty, so be prepared. Samantha's ultra crabby tonight. Even worse than she's usually been lately."

Mary grimaces. "Maybe we should just leave, El. We don't want to upset her."

"Come on, Mary," I remind her. "We should finish this now, shouldn't we?"

"I know, but somehow I felt braver this afternoon."

"Oh, don't worry," Ella says. "She's not going to bite you or anything. She might just tell us off and go to her room. She's in that kind of mood today."

Eesh. I can't even imagine what will happen when she sees *my* face.

"Our parents are gone out. We'll just go chill in the family room. She's in there now watching *Legally Blonde*."

"Oooh, I like that movie," I say. I follow closely behind the two of them as if I'm using them for protection.

Samantha is staring at the TV, and she looks miserable, as if she's not even seeing the screen. She glances up when we walk into the room and her face sags even more.

"What are *you* doing here?" she says.

I'm not sure who she's speaking to. Maybe just me, maybe all of us. I stifle the urge to turn and run.

"Thought we'd come and hang out here for a while and keep you company," Mary says in a soft voice.

"I don't need any company," Samantha says, standing up quickly. "I'm grounded, *remember* Ella? And I don't feel like talking to anybody, either."

Samantha pushes past us looking grim. I'm sure I see a flood of tears in her eyes.

"That worked well," Ella says as she flops down on the sofa. Then she sighs. "I don't even know what to do anymore. About *anything*. What a mess." She sighs, then sits there nibbling her lip, tapping her foot, and staring off into space.

Mary flops down beside her. "You must have some clue," she says. "You're her sister, after all. And you're twins. I thought twins had some sort of ESP or something. I thought you guys could practically read each other's minds."

"Not quite," Ella says, then rips open a bag of chips and starts munching.

I know what's wrong, I actually know, I feel like yelling out. *Samantha has the hots for Cole and she's done some rotten things! And now she feels totally guilty!* But I bite the words back because I'm not sure how blabbing to them would help us out right now. The sad thing is, though, our team is pretty much sunk for this year; there's no way we can possibly come close to winning unless Samantha and Ella sort their problems out.

We sit there watching the rest of the movie and none of us even laugh at the funny parts. We might as well just have the TV turned off. And we don't even see Samantha for the rest of the evening. I feel as if I'm sitting on an anthill, I'm so fidgety. *Should I tell them or shouldn't I? Should I? Shouldn't I?* are the only words that keep running through my head. It's a relief at 11:15 when Mary stands up.

"I have an eleven-thirty curfew," she says. "You ready to go, Daisy? We can walk home together."

"Sure!" I leap to my feet. I practically feel like racing her to the front door.

We both give Ella a little hug. Her eyes have filled with tears like her sister's did.

"Sorry it didn't work out," she says. "I hope this doesn't ruin our chances next Thursday. I'll try talking to her on the weekend, and tell her how important this is."

It's a perfect summer evening, even though it's not quite summer yet. Overhead there's a fingernail moon and pinpricks of starlight. Mary and I dawdle along, talking about Ella and Samantha. And finally, I let it all out, everything I know about the two of them, because I can't hold it in any longer. It's like I'm a pop bottle that somebody just shook, and everything comes fizzing out the top. I tell her about catching Samantha taping up the lock, how she blamed Ella for doing it, how I saw her with Cole in Tim's, and my suspicions about how crazy she is about him.

We're stopped under a street light. Mary's eyes are bugging out.

"Are you totally making this up or what, Daisy?"

"Why would I make it up? Haven't you noticed lately, the way Samantha stares at Ella and Cole when they're together? The way she keeps blaming everyone else for her problems? How weird she acts during track practice because Cole and Ella are there? It's like she's totally fixated on Cole, and I think the guilt is driving her crazy."

"Oh god, you're right. So what should we do?" Mary shakes her head.

"I'm not sure yet," I admit. "But something has to happen soon, or else the Vipers are totally sunk this year!"

When I finally reach home a little while later, I'm relieved to see Mom's car in the driveway. The light is on in Nate's room, so I know he's home, too, and I lock the door behind me. But when I reach the living room, I freeze. There's Dad, all curled up with a pillow and blanket, sleeping on the sofa!

He looks up at me bleary-eyed when he realizes I'm standing there staring at him.

"Hi honey," he says. "What time is it anyway?"

"Almost midnight," I tell him. "Why are you sleeping on the sofa, Dad?"

"Oh, I was just having trouble sleeping, tossing and turning," he mumbles. "Got a lot on my mind, some big decisions to make. Didn't want to disturb your mom. Good night, Daisy. Have a good sleep." He closes his eyes again.

Yeah right! Have a good sleep! Like that will happen now.

* * *

After a lousy sleep, tossing and turning because of what Dad told me last night, I can't even focus on homework the next day. I spend pretty much all of Saturday morning chatting online with Mary about the troubles with Ella and Samantha instead. And trying to come up with a way to fix everything. But how do you confront your so-called friend with such an awful accusation? We also spend time stewing about the track meet — we don't know how our team can possibly get past the heats with the way those blind passes have been going lately.

By lunchtime I know that I've already spent way

too long putting off my homework and studying for a French quiz next week. Mom and Dad are gone somewhere, but not together. They left before Nate even got up. Nate started questioning me about it when he finally showed up for breakfast. I tried my best not to sound upset and told him they'd gone out for breakfast, then to do some shopping. Nate took off to Austin's to make posters for the school play. It's really quiet around our place, but I still can't focus.

Maybe it's because I'm so worried about Mom. The truth is, she got all dressed up this morning and left the house with a smug smile on her face. She said she had to go to work, but she *never* works on a Saturday. And Dad said he needed to take a walk because he has so much to think about. They were both acting strange at breakfast this morning, too, just kept staring at each other in a weird way. I wonder what went on between them last night, and why Dad wound up on the sofa. I think I'm afraid to find out the truth.

After about half an hour I'm totally bored with studying. I'm feeling all jittery with worries, like I need to run so I can clear my head. So I get into some sweats, lace on my running shoes, and open the front door, just as a silver Mercedes Benz pulls into the driveway. At the same moment Dad is strolling along the sidewalk towards our house.

Then I realize that Mom is climbing out of the Mercedes. And getting out of the driver's seat is the hot guy that I saw her with in Tim Horton's!

I can't stop myself. I burst through the front door and straight into my mom's arms. Tears are already pouring down my cheeks just thinking of what's about to happen.

"Honey? What's *wrong?*" she says.

As if she doesn't know! Her hot boyfriend is standing there looking all puzzled and innocent. Dad's eyes, when he reaches us, are clouded with suspicion as he stares at both of them. Poor Dad! This is all falling apart so fast! Our poor family! I'm so frantic I can't even stop what blurts out of my mouth next.

"No, Mom! Please don't do it! Dad's not really a gambling addict. He was just giving it a try, and he didn't really lose any money either!"

"Daisy! What are you *talking* about?" Mom looks totally shocked, and a little embarrassed. So does Dad. His face is frozen with dismay. Maybe she didn't know about this side of Dad. Maybe this revelation is only making things worse for him. Then again, what *she* was doing the other day isn't much better.

"I *know* what you're up to, Mom," I tell her as I wipe away my tears. "I saw you that day in Tim's. *With him.*" I leer at the guy, who's not nearly as hot as he looks from a distance. Then I glance over at Dad with pity, but he's just standing there looking totally confused. I don't blame him. What a sad mess this is all becoming.

"Daisy, that's *enough*. I don't have a clue what you're

babbling about. This is Dr. McGraw, Glen," Mom announces, totally ignoring me now.

Oh great. She's ditching Dad for a doctor. How can poor Dad, the unemployed IT guy, possibly compete with a professional like *that?*

"I told you all about our plans last night at the restaurant. I hope you've had time to think about this. Because it's really time to hash this thing out now, Glen."

Oh no! Please Dad, don't agree to this!

Dad runs his fingers through his hair. He shakes his head as he stares at the two of them. A slow smile spreads over his face.

"Well if you can get past what Daisy just said and let me explain, then yes, I definitely think we should try this out and see if it works for all of us."

Then he walks over to Dr. McGraw and actually shakes his hand! I can't *believe* that he's giving Mom up to this guy so quickly.

"Don't you have a conscience?" I say to Mom and her doctor. Then I run over to stand beside Dad and hang onto his arm to show him my support. "What about *us?* What about me and Nate? And poor Dad! How could you do this to him?"

Mom's face is a blank mask now. She's frowning as she stares at me. Then her eyes open wide and she actually starts smiling.

"Daisy." She pauses. "Dr. McGraw is starting a new walk-in medical clinic and he needs some office help, nursing staff, and a data entry consultant, someone to get the whole system set up for him. He wants to give your dad a job. *That's* what this is about."

"Pardon?" I'm not sure I've heard right.

When I look at Dad, he's grinning. Dr. McGraw is grinning too. Then the three of them begin to laugh!

"Daisy, shouldn't you find something else to obsess about?" Dad says. "Like *running* maybe? Aren't you on a track team or something?" But he's laughing so hard he can barely even get the words out.

"Well I'm glad you all find this so hilarious," I tell them. Then I spin around and stomp inside the house, wishing I had the power to make myself invisible.

★ ★ ★

I hide out in my room for the rest of the afternoon because I'm too ashamed to face everyone. Especially Dr. McGraw, the nice man who is offering my dad a job. Mom has made coffee — I can smell it — and I can hear their voices from the kitchen where they're in a deep discussion about this new clinic. Thank goodness that's all it was!

Maybe, like Dad said, I should just think less and run more, because now I can't even figure out how I wound up so far off track. I guess it was easy enough, with the way Mom and Dad have been treating each other lately. I'm so glad I finally have that puzzle solved.

Sometimes you can just worry way too much for no reason at all!

That doesn't stop me from obsessing about Finn, though, which is really nothing unusual when it comes to *that* guy. Thoughts of Finn pop up on me constantly, like text messages from my brain! It doesn't stop me from worrying about our relay team either. What will happen at the meet next week? Will we even be a team by then?

But Saturday evening, oh, Saturday evening! We all go out together as a family and splurge on a huge Chinese food dinner. We haven't done this in ages. Mom and Dad sit close together in the booth across from Nate and me. Their arms are touching and they seem to be enjoying the closeness. Every time I glance up from my food and see them sitting there, I feel all warm and cozy inside. Nate doesn't even notice. He has his face in his plate the entire time, inhaling his Kung Pao Chicken and spring rolls.

9 TRACKING DOWN THE TRUTH

I'm feeling pretty smug by Monday morning. That's because I slept so well for a change on Saturday night, and got all caught up with my assignments on Sunday. And joy of joys, Madame doesn't have to yell at me once for falling asleep in class. In fact, she even congratulates me for answering a couple of questions correctly. Which puts me on cloud nine for the rest of the day.

At lunchtime Ella and Samantha are sitting at opposite ends of the cafeteria. Mary and I put our heads together and come to the conclusion that after what happened at their place on Friday night, things are probably worse than they were when track practice ended last week. Now they're not even speaking. This can't be good, but I don't let it spoil my mood. Mom and Dad are going to make it after all! Yay!

But by the time I reach the track for practice after school, my whole mood changes. The first thing I realize is that there's no sign of Finn. Almost everyone else is out there by the time three o'clock rolls around. Every time I hear the school doors slam open I check to see if it's Finn. Then the two coaches come sauntering out of the school with their clipboards to tell us today's plan, and I know Finn is doomed. Coach Polito wants everyone out here on the track by the time she arrives. And Finn is still nowhere in sight. I turn to glance at Mary and she's watching the school doors, wide-eyed. Ella is squashed up against Cole, as usual. And Samantha is watching, too, scanning the other athletes.

Huh! Pretending she's looking for Finn, quite clearly. Please, don't tell me that she's done the tape trick again! And now the coach is looking around herself.

"Finn Sinclair," she calls out. She doesn't get an answer and her face goes hard.

"That's it, last chance," I hear her tell Coach Jensen. My stomach drops like I'm on an elevator.

Finn shows up a few minutes later, comes running full speed out of the school and stands in front of the coach, panting.

"I can explain, Coach," he gasps.

Her face is blank. She doesn't even acknowledge that he's standing there. She just calls Wyatt over, right in front of Finn.

"Can you fill in for Finn Sinclair for this season, Wyatt?" she says to him. "Finn seems to have ditched the team. I guess he has better things to do."

Wyatt stands there dumbfounded. "I . . . I guess so," he says, staring straight at Finn now. "But I think maybe if you let him —"

"That's great, Wyatt," Coach says. "I knew you'd be on board. Positions please, boys' relay teams." Then she just turns around and walks away.

Everyone is staring at Finn. Josh and Langdon look stunned at this announcement, and I can't help but notice the way they're staring at Cole. Finn is standing there, arms hanging limply at his sides, and watching the back of the coach. Then he heads towards the school doors as if he has weights on his ankles. I turn to look at Samantha. She's looking at Ella, and Ella is looking at Cole. And Cole has the biggest grin on his face right now. He pats Wyatt on the back.

"Way to go, buddy," he says. "This totally rocks. Maybe not so much for Finn right now, though." He raises a smug eyebrow then makes a sad face. "Tough break."

I think there might be steam blowing out of my ears! This is so awful, I can barely even stand it. Poor Finn! I feel like running after him and wrapping him in a huge hug. I feel like shouting at the coach that it's not his fault at all. Why won't he just shout it out himself? How can a piece of duct tape get you kicked off a track team?

I'm just about to do it, to go running after Finn and talk him into telling Coach the truth, when a sudden sob bursts out of the crowd of kids, and everyone looks over. Ella has jumped to her feet, and she's running now towards the school. Then Samantha jumps up and goes running towards the entrance right behind her sister. And she's crying, too.

"Mary and Daisy," Coach Polito nods at us. "Maybe you should go and find out what's up with those two . . ."

Before she can even finish her sentence, though, we're both on our feet running after our friends. When we find them in the change room, Ella has locked herself in a stall and Samantha is standing outside trying to talk to her.

"Please come out," she's saying as Mary and I watch. "Let's talk about this now. I'm your *sister*. Come on, Ella. Listen to me. *Please!*"

It looks as if Samantha is finally going to tell her sister the truth about her mad crush on Cole. What a relief. Maybe they can get this all straightened out and salvage what's left of our team. She turns and looks at us for a moment, and scrubs the tears from her own face. Clearly this nasty turn of events with Finn has her upset.

"Maybe she has a heart after all," I whisper to Mary, and she nods hopefully.

We hear a click. Then the door swings open and Ella steps out. When she spots me and Mary standing there, she bursts into tears again.

"How could I have been so stupid?" Ella sobs. "How did this all happen, Samantha?"

Samantha turns and looks at me. "Why don't you ask

Daisy," she says, pointing in my direction. "Tell her everything you know, Daisy. I just can't *take* this anymore."

"Are you sure, Samantha?" I ask her. Samantha just sniffs and nods.

And yet again I get stuck trying to explain things. The whole time I'm talking about the duct tape and how they blamed each other, Ella's chin is quivering as she watches Samantha's face. Samantha is completely devastated, judging by how wide her mouth and eyes are open. And I haven't even gotten to the worst part of the story yet!

When I reach the part about Tim Horton's, and how Samantha was with Cole impersonating Ella that day, Ella's eyes flood with tears, and she starts to sob even harder than Samantha. What a complete and utter mess this whole thing has become!

"Really, I don't know how you can even live with yourself, Ella, after what just happened out there!" Samantha says between sobs. "Especially knowing that Cole is the biggest jerk in the world — did you see how he reacted when Finn got cut from the team just now."

Huh? What is Samantha talking about? Am I hearing right? Samantha blows her nose in a piece of toilet paper, then keeps right on talking, but saying nothing I expected to hear!

"I mean, everybody else seems to know what he's like except *you*. Or maybe you were just ignoring it. But why would you ever think of doing this stuff to *me?* Why would you lie about the duct tape to Daisy, Ella? Why would you let her believe that I was the one who did that to Finn?"

Wait, what? Ella was the one who was lying all along? Ella taped up the lock? *Uh oh.* When I glance over at Mary, she's staring at me and frowning.

"But you did it to me, *too*," Ella says. "Why would you do that to *me?* Why would you even sneak around with Cole?" Then she spins around and heads for the door.

"Because I *care* about you," I hear Samantha murmur in a hoarse voice as Ella is walking away. "I just *faked* being you so I could find out more about him. I was going to tell you about going to Tim's with Cole eventually, but it all just got so complicated."

That's when it dawns on me, and now my eyes and mouth are open wide, too. I've just realized something that I can hardly believe. I was *totally* wrong about Samantha *and* Ella!

"Wait," I yell, and Ella stops with her hand on the door knob. "Don't you get it? So Samantha actually did it *for* you, Ella! She knows what Cole is like, and she was trying to protect you so you won't get your heart broken. Am I right, Samantha?"

Samantha is standing there nodding. "And I knew that *you* knew that, too, Daisy. And it made me sick inside, and I couldn't figure out a way to fix it all without Ella getting hurt. Like I said, I was trying to find out more when I was pretending to be Ella that day."

"That's really messed up, you guys," Mary says.

"I *know!*" Samantha is nodding and sniffling now. "And I found out that Ella was taping up Finn's lock so Cole would like her even more, because the jerk actually thanked me for doing it that day in Tim's when he thought I was Ella! He's such a *loser.* He kept saying that he wished Finn hadn't shown up this year, how he doesn't deserve to be on the team. And that I should try taping the lock up one more time to try and get him kicked off for good. I couldn't stand that Ella was hung up on such a creep. That she would try to help get Finn kicked off the team."

Now Samantha is sobbing and hiccupping. And Ella has turned around slowly. Something in her face has softened, and she's blinking quickly, swallowing her sobs.

"You were really doing all that for *me?*" she asks, walking towards her sister.

"Uh-*huh,*" Samantha says, nodding and sniffling. "And I *know* I was being such a jerk at home, and Mom and Dad are mad at me, too, but it was so hard to walk around knowing what Cole was really like, and hiding it from you!"

"Oh god, Samantha, you were so right," Ella blurts out. "I did it for stupid Cole. I thought he'd like me better — I was so afraid he might pick you instead. He flirts with everyone, and I was willing to do whatever he wanted so that he'd choose me."

"Even risk getting caught doing something so

stupid?" Samantha shakes her head. "And helping get a teammate kicked off the team. Jeez, Ella! What were you even thinking?"

"Well obviously I wasn't! When I knew Daisy had spotted me taping the lock that day, I blurted out a lie to her and said that I saw you doing it. And I've been trying to live with this and it's been driving me crazy!" Ella pauses and her whole body seems to sag. "And then I went and did it again today. Just because Cole wanted me to. God!"

Samantha reaches out, wraps Ella in her arms and starts hugging her hard. Ella is startled for a second, then starts hugging her sister right back. They're both kind of laughing and crying at the same time, and whispering in each other's ears. It's amazing, really, this sisterly love of theirs. I must remember to try and be more patient with Nate.

Mary leans towards me. "I can't *believe* how much you knew all along," she says.

I can't believe how much I didn't know until just now, I'm thinking. "Well you know, Mary, you can't always control *everything*," I tell her. "Sometimes you just have to leave a problem alone and somehow it'll work itself out."

"You know something?" Mary says, grinning at me. "I never thought I'd hear *you* say something like that in this lifetime."

"Me neither," I confess with a sheepish smile.

10 A RUNNING START

By the time we're headed back out to the field a few minutes later, Ella and Samantha have both splashed their faces with cold water and made a vow that the Vipers will reign supreme this year. But there's still that niggling question. Why hasn't anyone mentioned to Ella that she should 'fess up to Coach about how she's the one responsible for getting Finn booted off the team? It's eating away at me as we're wandering through the hallway towards the exit. I can't help myself. I have to say it out loud.

"Ella?"

She stops with her hand on the door and turns to look at me.

"Aren't you forgetting something? What about Finn? He's kicked off the track team because of you."

"Oh god, that's right," she says, then slaps a hand over her mouth.

"You have to tell Coach," I say in a quiet voice. "You have to do the right thing, Ella. For Finn's sake."

Mary and Samantha are standing there nodding in agreement with me. Right away, Ella's eyes well up with tears again.

"But then I'll get booted off our team," she says then swallows loudly. "And then I won't be one of the Vipers anymore."

Mary and Samantha aren't nodding anymore. They're looking from Ella to me, then back again at Ella.

"That would totally suck," Samantha says, crooking her arm through Ella's. "We've worked so hard for this! Maybe she could confess after the meet. So we don't mess up the team."

"But Finn's worked hard, too," I insist. "He deserves to run, don't you think? This just doesn't feel right, you guys."

"Well it feels right to me," Samantha says, then drags Ella out the doors into the blinking bright daylight.

I can hardly believe it and stand there squinting with a huge lump in my throat. Mary pats me on the back.

"You did your best, Daisy," she says. "And honestly, I don't even know what to think about all this anymore."

"But you're on my side, right?" I say. "You think she should tell."

"It would be the right thing to do, I guess," she says, then sighs.

I follow the rest of my team outside. The boys' teams are having another run-through and they're all set up in their lanes around the track. Four sets of runners waiting for that pistol to go off so that they can take off. The coach is at the finish line with her pistol in the air. The first runners are crouched in starting position.

"Runners take your marks . . . Get set . . ." BANG!

When the gun goes off, my heart leaps, as usual. As I watch Langdon take off, my heart starts pumping as if I'm running myself. Langdon makes a perfect blind pass to Josh, and of course, they're way ahead of the grade six and seven runners. Josh is rounding the curve, and Cole has his hand sticking out behind him, ready to feel it slap his palm. They're doing amazing. When I look over at Coach, she's smiling broadly for a change. Cole takes off down the straightaway, headed for Wyatt who's waiting at the curve to get his hands on that baton. Then to charge for the finish line. And what, I wonder, is Finn doing right now? The guy who should be standing where Wyatt is.

Cole has almost reached Wyatt when it happens. He stumbles suddenly, then wipes out on the track and skids face down on the gravel! Even though it all happens so fast, it still feels like slow motion. The grade sixes and sevens go pounding past him. Cole just lies motionless in his face plant, not moving a muscle.

In an instant he's surrounded by the two coaches and everyone else on his team. The rest of the runners all gather, too, and stand grim-faced in a circle around him. Coach Jensen has him up on his feet in a couple of seconds. Cole is wincing, and there's a huge gash on both of his knees, rivulets of blood trickling down his hairy legs.

"Wow," he says, trying to laugh it off. "I sure didn't see that coming."

"You might need stitches," Coach Polito tells him. "Maybe not in both knees, but one of them looks pretty bad. Think you can take him to the emergency room so they can pick out the gravel and clean him up, Coach Jensen?" she asks.

"Sure thing," the coach says.

"Stitches?" Cole has gone dead pale. He almost looks as if he might puke. "I've never had stitches before." He tries to muster up a smile, but he looks on the verge of tears. And for a split second, I feel like laughing out loud. Is that karma or what?

We all stand there watching as Cole goes limping off the field with his arm around Coach Jensen's shoulder for support. Coach Polito is standing there shaking her head. She doesn't look thrilled at all.

"Well," she says. "So much for the grade eight boys' relay team winning this year. We'll have to find another sub, since we've lost our two fastest guys."

Josh, Wyatt, and Langdon's faces drop. Oh god, this can't be happening. I glance over at Ella. Mary and Samantha are staring at her now, too. Will she or won't she? She looks up at the sky and down at her shoes. Then she looks over at me. She's blinking fast, trying to hold back her tears. Then she takes a slow step forward.

"Coach Polito?" she murmurs, touching Coach's

arm. "Can I talk to you for a second?"

"Right now, Ella?" Coach says. "To be honest, I almost feel like tearing out my hair right about now, so this had better be important."

"Oh, I think it probably is," Ella says, then leads the surprised coach away by the arm, out into the middle of the field to talk.

Mary, Samantha, and I stand there, watching and waiting.

★ ★ ★

It's always nerve-wracking before a race. Those butterflies in my stomach are fluttering out of control and my blood feels as if it's surging through my veins. I have to keep running in place to try to relieve some of the tension. I shake out my hands and legs too, and try to stay calm. It happens every single time, including today, right at this very moment. And then I hear those words.

"Runners take your marks . . . Get set . . ." BANG.

When the cap pistol goes off, Mary practically explodes from the starting blocks. She's flying along the track like a gazelle, her long mane trailing behind her. She makes a perfect blind pass to Inez, who starts churning up the gravel around the curve, now heading towards Samantha. Then I hear her yell the magic word, "stick!" Samantha has the baton after another perfect pass.

Every atom of my being is vibrating as my moment approaches. I watch over my shoulder as Samantha comes charging towards me with a huge grin on her face, then I turn to look straight ahead the way I'm supposed to, and wait. And then I hear it. "*Stick*," as the baton slaps my hand. I'm madly dashing for the finish, my arms and legs pumping like pistons, everything around me a blur. I swoop across it and fling my arms in the air and start waving that baton around as my teammates run up to join me.

"Nicely done, girls," a beaming Coach Polito tells us all. "That was just *great*, for a change. I can't believe how much your time and technique have improved since last week. You've cleaned up this race. Too bad nobody else was racing against you today!" she adds, then throws back her head and laughs.

We all look at each other, Mary, Inez, Samantha, and I, and start laughing right along with our coach. Then we all start giving each other high-fives. Now we finally have a functioning team again, and it feels great!

"You think *this* was good, Coach," I tell her, smacking her hand in the air. "Just wait until the track meet on Thursday!"

I glance towards the bleachers where Ella is sitting watching us. She's even wearing her Vipers t-shirt in support of our team. She waves, and gives me the thumbs-up sign, and I give it right back to her. Inez might not be as fast as Ella, but she's pretty close. And that makes all of us happy, especially our coach.

I'm proud of what Ella did on Monday, resigning from the team because of what she did to Finn, then telling Coach that Inez should take her place. When Cole heard about it, after he got stitched up, he faked his astonishment. He couldn't believe that Ella would do anything so dumb to Finn. He said he was only kidding when he told Samantha at Timmy's that day, thinking she was Ella, that he wanted the lock taped up again. He asked her why she always took everything seriously. And she just shrugged at him and walked away.

I was proud of her for doing that, too. She should have done it a long time ago. She's suspended from the team until after the meet on Thursday, which is tomorrow. Yikes! Then she and Coach are going to get together to discuss ways of fixing things between Ella and the rest of the team. She thinks maybe they can work something out, find a way for her to gain back everyone's trust. Maybe Coach Polito has a heart after all, too. My fingers are crossed, anyway.

Finn comes loping across the field, and *omigawd*, he's running right towards me. My heart picks up speed, as usual. He can't stop talking about what happened two days ago. He needs to keep telling me how sorry he is every chance he gets.

"Great race, Daze," he says and offers me a high-five, which I gladly return. "You guys will do amazing tomorrow. Trust me, I just know it. Inez is a machine when she needs to be."

Then he stands there staring at me, and I'm feeling warm all over because there's a new look in his chocolate-brown eyes that I've never seen before. When he puts his hands on my shoulders I practically start to dissolve.

"Jeez, Daze," he says, staring right into my eyes. "I've gotta say it again. I'm *so sorry* I didn't believe you last week. But you have to admit it looked like I caught you in the act when I found you with my lock in your hand. I was so blown away that I just had to walk away. You should have phoned me or something. You should have tried to explain everything. But you seemed to be avoiding me."

"Well I thought you were avoiding *me*," I tell him, then I sigh. If only I'd tried to talk to him again instead of wasting so much time stewing about it. But I had a lot of other stuff on my mind last week, all of which has finally worked itself out.

Things have never been better at home with Dad out working again instead of losing money online. I know I'll still have to cook dinner half the time, but I think I'm actually starting to like it. Nate will eat anything I put on his plate anyway, he's always so grateful when there's food waiting for him after drama rehearsals. And I'm so glad I didn't have to break his heart about Samantha. He was right to trust her after all, and he was sure to tell me that after he heard the whole crazy story. Honestly, it's such a relief knowing that I can finally sleep again at night instead of worrying so much about everything and everyone. I finally realized it — worrying doesn't change a single thing!

Then something amazing happens. Finn wraps his arms around me and hugs me hard. And kisses me right on the nose!

"Honestly, I'm *really* sorry," he says close to my ear. I just about melt into a puddle on the spot.

I know it's not a lip kiss, but I'd say it's a running start!